D1123720

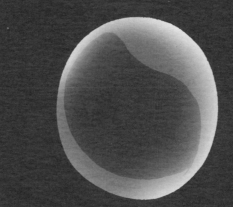

Discarded from
Garfield County Public
Library System

GARFIELD COUNTY LIBRARIES
Carbondale Branch Library
320 Sopris Ave
Carbondale, CO 81623
(970) 963-2889 – Fax (970) 963-8573
www.gcpld.org

There's a Witch

IN YOUR BOOK

Written by TOM FLETCHER

Illustrated by GREG ABBOTT

Random House 🏠 New York

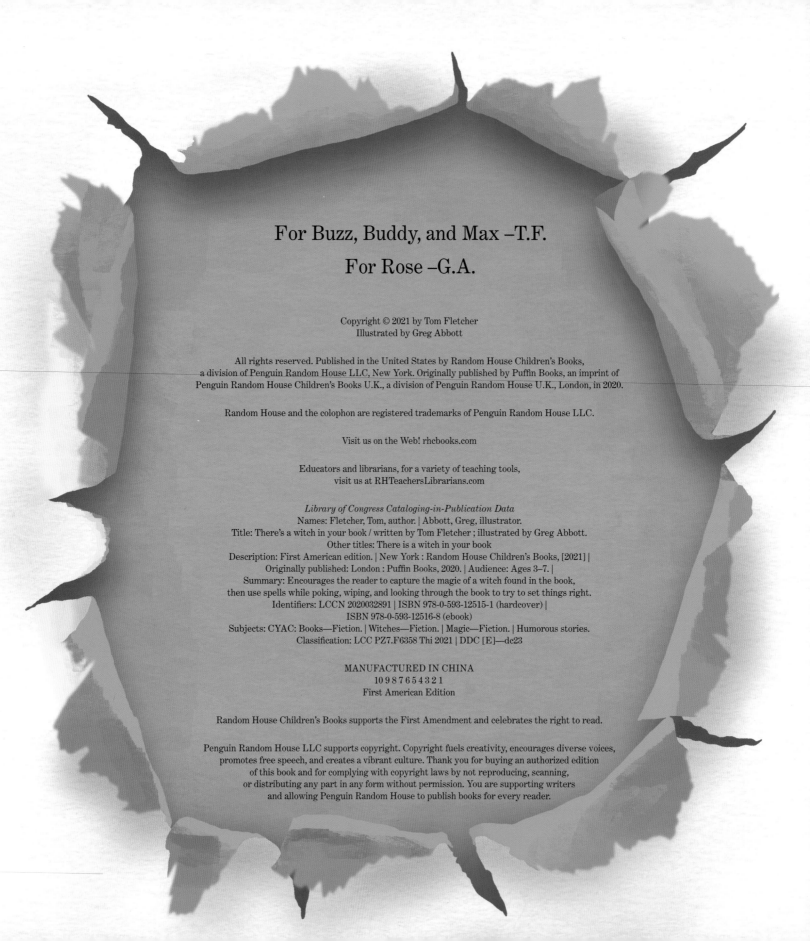

For Buzz, Buddy, and Max –T.F.

For Rose –G.A.

Copyright © 2021 by Tom Fletcher
Illustrated by Greg Abbott

All rights reserved. Published in the United States by Random House Children's Books,
a division of Penguin Random House LLC, New York. Originally published by Puffin Books, an imprint of
Penguin Random House Children's Books U.K., a division of Penguin Random House U.K., London, in 2020.

Random House and the colophon are registered trademarks of Penguin Random House LLC.

Visit us on the Web! rhcbooks.com

Educators and librarians, for a variety of teaching tools,
visit us at RHTeachersLibrarians.com

Library of Congress Cataloging-in-Publication Data
Names: Fletcher, Tom, author. | Abbott, Greg, illustrator.
Title: There's a witch in your book / written by Tom Fletcher ; illustrated by Greg Abbott.
Other titles: There is a witch in your book
Description: First American edition. | New York : Random House Children's Books, [2021] |
Originally published: London : Puffin Books, 2020. | Audience: Ages 3–7. |
Summary: Encourages the reader to capture the magic of a witch found in the book,
then use spells while poking, wiping, and looking through the book to try to set things right.
Identifiers: LCCN 2020032891 | ISBN 978-0-593-12515-1 (hardcover) |
ISBN 978-0-593-12516-8 (ebook)
Subjects: CYAC: Books—Fiction. | Witches—Fiction. | Magic—Fiction. | Humorous stories.
Classification: LCC PZ7.F6358 Thi 2021 | DDC [E]—dc23

MANUFACTURED IN CHINA
10 9 8 7 6 5 4 3 2 1
First American Edition

Random House Children's Books supports the First Amendment and celebrates the right to read.

Penguin Random House LLC supports copyright. Copyright fuels creativity, encourages diverse voices,
promotes free speech, and creates a vibrant culture. Thank you for buying an authorized edition
of this book and for complying with copyright laws by not reproducing, scanning,
or distributing any part in any form without permission. You are supporting writers
and allowing Penguin Random House to publish books for every reader.

EEEK!
There's a **WITCH** in your book!

What a **mess** she's making!

Wipe the mess away, and turn the page.

Well done! You cleaned up the mess!

But—**UH-OH**—now Witch looks cross.
I don't think she likes us unmuddling her mess.

WATCH OUT!

She's about to turn you into a toad!
Quickly, **hold up your hand** to block the spell. . . .

Phew!
You caught the magic in your hand.

What a cheeky witch! Let's teach her a lesson
and turn *her* into something instead.

Use your finger as a **magic wand**,
and say these words:

Magic this, magic that,
Turn this witch into a cat!

The spell worked!
You turned the witch into a stinky little cat!

But look—she has **fleas**!
And they're hopping all over your book.

Use your **magic wand finger**,
and say this spell:

Magic silly, magic funny,
Turn each flea into a . . . bunny!

OH NO! We didn't think that through.
Now your book is **full of bunnies!**

Okay, I know just the spell to get rid of bunnies.
Finger wands ready:

Magic far, magic near,
Make the bunnies disappear!

WHOOPS!

Those bunnies are *see-through* now,
but they're **STILL IN YOUR BOOK!**

Now they're **bubble bunnies**!

Hmm—try **poking** all the bubbles
with your **magic wand finger**. . . .

Aaargh!

Those bubbles were full of slime!

Now your book is *even messier*
than it was before.

Oh dear! This has all gone horribly wrong.
If only we knew someone
who could put everything right. . . .

Oh yes! **WITCH**, of course!
Do you think she might be more helpful this time?

Let's try turning that stinky little cat
back into a witch.

Finger wands up!

Magic scratch, magic itch,
Turn the cat into a witch!

Great—Witch is back!

And I think she has
a spell to help us. . . .

Will this clean up the slime?

WiZWHACKEROO!!

Ooooh!
Her spell made a hole in your book.

And she has a plan. . . .

...nd to help Witch swoosh all the slime through the hole....

Done! Your book is all tidy.
Thank you, Witch.

a minute. . . .

swooshed the slime through the hole,
t mean that now your room is messy!

Take a peek through the hole at your room. . . .

PHEW! I can't see any slime, but I do think your room could be a bit don't you?

(And when you tidy up, please—**NO MAGIC SPELLS!**)

Now you have such a tidy book,
I think it's time for a spooky sleepover.

Shall we do **ONE MORE SPELL?**

Yes!

Use your **magic wand finger** to make some spooky sleepover guests appear!

Magic snoozy, magic dozy,
Call some friends, and let's get cozy!

It worked!

Have a fun sleepover, little spooks. . . .
(Try not to make *too* much mess!)

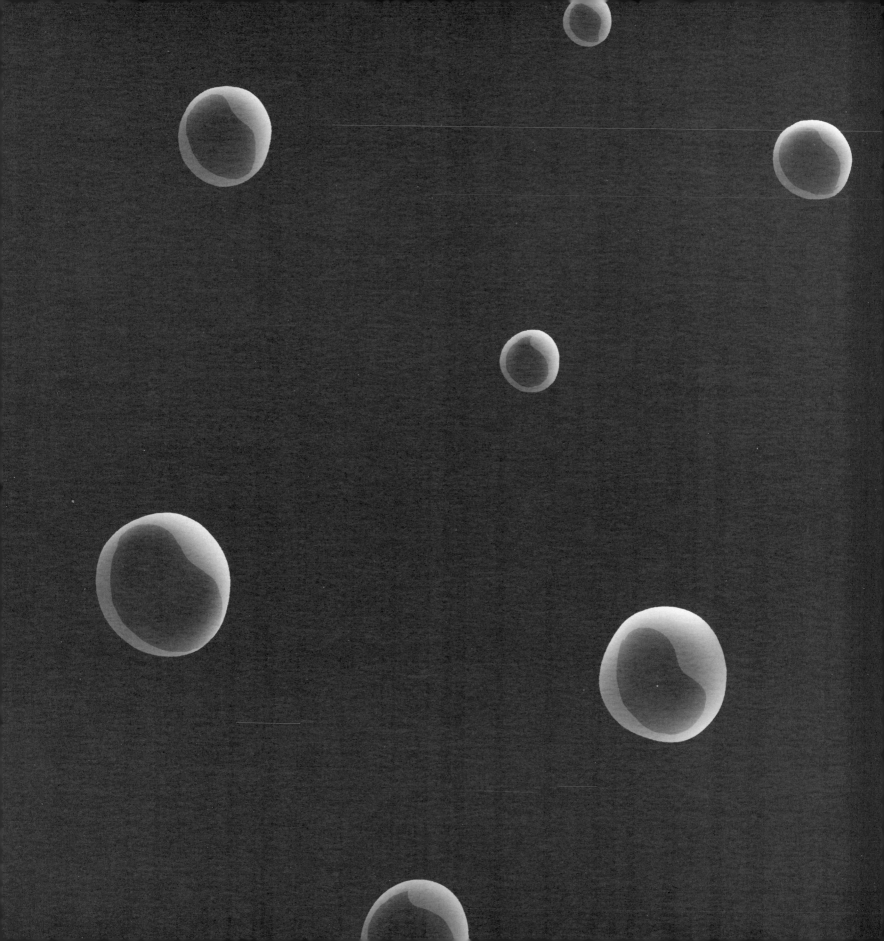